My "d" Sound Box®

(Blends are included in this book.)

Library of Congress Cataloging-in-Publication Data
Moncure, Jane Belk.
My "d" sound box / by Jane Belk Moncure; illustrated by Colin King.
p. cm.
Summary: A little girl fills her sound box with many words that begin with the letter "d."
ISBN 1-56766-770-8 (lib. bdg. : alk. paper)
[1. Alphabet.] I. King, Colin, ill. II. Title.
PZ7.M739 Myd 2000
[E]—dc21   99-055408

My "d" Sound Box

Jane Belk Moncure

illustrated by Colin King

The Child's World

Little  had a box.

"I will find things that begin
with my 'd' sound," she said.

"I will put them into
my sound  box."

Little  found dolls.

She found all kinds of dolls,

dolls, dolls!

One doll danced.

One doll played a drum.

Did Little  d put the dolls into her box? She did.

But some dolls fell out.

So Little  said,

"I will turn this box into a dollhouse for the dolls and me!"

And she did.

Little  made doll

desks . . .

and doll dressers.

She put them in the dollhouse.

She made a dining room with a table

and dishes  for the table.

Little  made doll dresses,

all kinds of doll dresses.

Then she dressed her dolls . . .

and took them for a drive in the desert.

They saw a dromedary.

Little 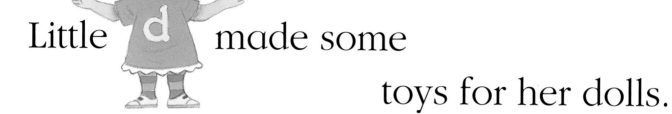 made some

toys for her dolls.

She made ducks

for some dolls.

She made dogs for some dolls.

She put the ducks and dogs
into the dollhouse.

One day, a doll was sick.

So she took the doll to a   doctor.

One day, a doll had a toothache.

So Little  took the doll

 to a  dentist.

One day, Little  opened
the door

and found a dollar

and a dime.

"I will buy  for my dolls,"
she said.

"We will have donuts for dinner."

She put a dozen donuts on the dining room table.

donuts

dolls

dog

Why did she need a dozen?

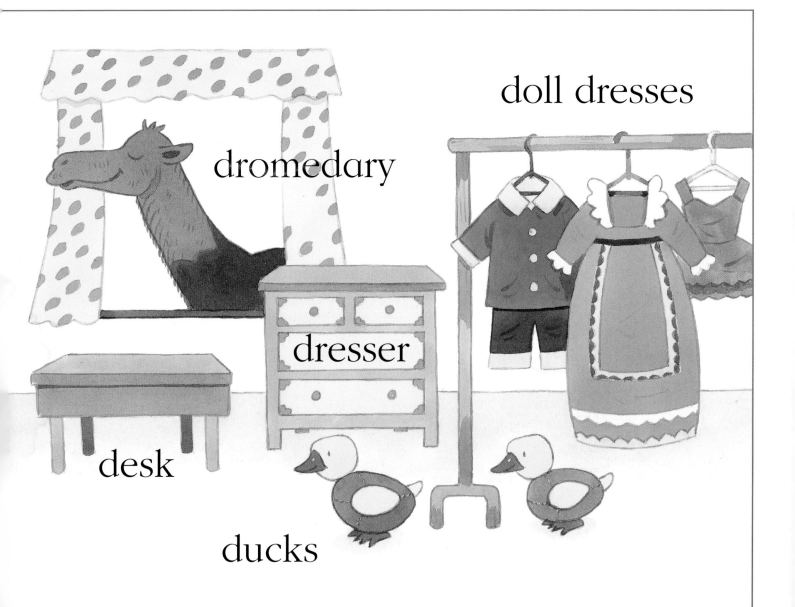

dromedary

doll dresses

dresser

desk

ducks

Can you read these words

with Little  ?

diamond

 domino

 diary

 daisy

deer

dwarf

dustpan

dove

donkey

dandelion

doghouse

dinosaur

ABOUT THE AUTHOR AND ILLUSTRATOR

Jane Belk Moncure began her writing career when she was in kindergarten. She has never stopped writing. Many of her children's stories and poems have been published, to the delight of young readers, including her son Jim, whose childhood experiences found their way into many of her books.

Mrs. Moncure's writing is based upon an active career in early childhood education.
A recipient of an M.A. degree from Columbia University, Mrs. Moncure has taught and directed nursery, kindergarten, and primary grade programs in California, New York, Virginia, and North Carolina. As a former member of the faculties of Virginia Commonwealth University and the University of Richmond, she taught prospective teachers in early childhood education.

Mrs. Moncure has travelled extensively abroad, studying early childhood programs in the United Kingdom, The Netherlands, and Switzerland. She was the first president of the Virginia Association for Early Childhood Education and received its award for outstanding service to young children.

A resident of North Carolina, Mrs. Moncure is currently a full-time writer and educational consultant. She is married to Dr. James A. Moncure, former vice president of Elon College.

Colin King studied at the Royal College of Art, London. He started his freelance career as an illustrator, working for magazines and advertising agencies.

He began drawing pictures for children's books in 1976 and has illustrated over sixty titles to date.

Included in a wide variety of subjects are a best-selling children's encyclopedia and books about spies and detectives.

His books have been translated into several languages, including Japanese and Hebrew. He has four grown-up children and lives in Suffolk, England, with his wife, three dogs, and a cat.